DATE DUE			
MAY 22 '95			

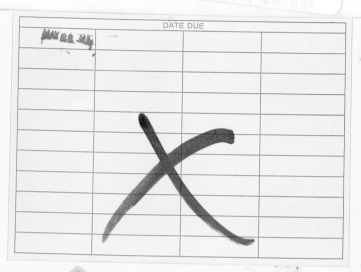

BTSB Bound to Stay Bound Books, Inc.

THE
TORMENTORS

THE
TORMENTORS

LYNN HALL

Harcourt Brace Jovanovich, Publishers

San Diego   New York   London

HBJ

Copyright © 1990 by Lynn Hall

4/15/91 BTSB 14.95

Requests for permission to make copies of any
part of the work should be mailed to:
Permissions Department,
Harcourt Brace Jovanovich, Publishers,
Orlando, Florida 32887.

Library of Congress Cataloging-in-Publication Data
Hall, Lynn.
The tormentors/by Lynn Hall.
p. cm.
Summary: When his beloved German shepherd vanishes, Sox sets
out to find the thief and finds himself involved with a ring of dangerous
dog trainers who kidnap animals for their own illegal profit.
ISBN 0-15-289470-5
[1. Dogs—Fiction. 2. Crime—Fiction. 3. Mystery and detective stories.] I. Title.
PZ7.H1458Tp 1990
[Fic]—dc20 90-4805

Printed in the United States of America

First edition

A B C D E

Other books by Lynn Hall

Murder in a Pig's Eye

In Trouble *Again*, Zelda Hammersmith?

Zelda Strikes Again!

Here Comes Zelda Claus
and Other Holiday Disasters

Flyaway

The Solitary

If Winter Comes

Mrs. Portree's Pony

The Giver

Tazo and Me

The Secret Life of Dagmar Schultz

Dagmar Schultz and the Powers of Darkness

Dagmar Schultz and the Green-eyed Monster

Dagmar Schultz and the Angel Edna

1

My real name is Cesare but none of my friends know that. I got the nickname of Sox when I was little, because I was always wearing socks that didn't match.

I don't care. It's more American than Cesare. All us kids were born right here in Albuquerque, but Mama is Hispanic and Dad is German so people get confused sometimes. I can see why, with five kids named Cesare, Hans, Ricardo, Luther, and Cruzita.

But then our whole neighborhood is pretty much like that. We live on the south edge of Albuquerque, between Highway 47 and the Rio Grande. The houses are mostly small and square and flat-roofed, with lots of security fences and watchdogs, and cars being rebuilt or torn apart under the backyard trees.

The day the trouble started, I was sitting on our back step with Heidi, half watching Hans and Jeraldo, half thinking my own thoughts. Heidi lay flat on the ground, panting and twitching the end of her tail. She was dreaming; I could tell by the way her closed eyelids moved.

She was the best dog in the neighborhood. No, in the world. She was a pure black German shepherd, three years old, and she was mine even before she was born. Her mother belonged to my Uncle Luis, down in Las Lunas. I used to sit beside that pregnant dog and put my hand on her belly and feel little puppy knees and elbows and heads moving around in there.

Mama and Dad had already said I could buy one of the pups, but I had to pay full price, one hundred dollars, and I had to earn it myself. That was the deal. That was to make sure I really wanted a dog bad enough, and would appreciate her afterwards. Also, it was because Uncle Luis needed the money and couldn't afford to give away hundred-dollar puppies.

I was only eleven then, and it wasn't easy finding ways to earn money. Some places maybe a kid could mow lawns, but here all we got for lawns is rock and maybe cactus. Nothing to mow in our neighborhood, and if there was, the mean dogs behind the fences would trample it all to death before it got high enough to mow.

I washed cars and ran errands all summer to get that hundred dollars. I could have got it easy and fast by selling joints of marijuana at school. Hans's buddy Jeraldo was in the business already and he was only sixteen. But I was scared of getting started in that stuff. So I went to the store for Mrs. Murillo when she broke her hip, and washed about a million cars, and earned my dog.

I wanted a male, but there were only females in the litter. I picked Heidi because she was pure black, and the others were black and brown mixed. Ever since I was little I'd had the feeling that I was different from everybody else, especially my brothers, but I didn't know exactly how, or whether it was good-different or bad-different. Just sort of . . . separate. And I wanted a dog who would be separate with me, you know what I mean? Those other guys were always having to prove something, how good they were at whatever they were doing, or how tough they were, or how brave. I already knew I wasn't any of those things. I guess I was just trying to figure out how to get through life as I was, while they were trying to con people into thinking they were more than they really were.

I sat on the back step watching the shadow of the house move out from the wall by slow inches as the afternoon got late. It was June, with daylight till almost nine and not a cloud in the whole turquoise sky—not a breath of air moving.

Ahead of me, a whole summer of hot, still, empty days to fill up before school started again. Even though I didn't admit it to my friends, I liked school. At least I liked having someplace to be at a certain time, with a definite job in front of me. Read chapter ten. Work the problems on page ninety. I liked the coolness of the school air-conditioning, and I liked the lunches.

What I hated about school was being away from Heidi, and knife fights. I'd never been in one yet. I didn't even carry a knife. But one of my worst fears was of getting knifed. They said it didn't hurt when the blade sliced through your skin, that it only hurt afterwards. But I couldn't stand the thought, anyhow.

That's why I sat there on the back step trying not to pay attention to Hans and Jeraldo. Jeraldo had got cut up by one of his customers—another reason I didn't want to get into the marijuana-selling business.

Hans slammed down the hood of his pickup and dumped the used motor oil and empty oilcans behind the garage, where he dumped everything. Jeraldo said he had business to take care of, and peeled away in his big old Plymouth with the fenders that didn't match. Hans stood over me and Heidi and rested one foot on Heidi's head, teasing.

Hans was short and square-built, dark like Mama but with Dad's blue eyes. All five of us had different combinations of Mama, tiny and dark, and Dad, huge and blond. Cruzi and Luther were tall; Hans and Ric, short. I was the youngest—too early to tell about me yet. Uncle Luis would take my arm and measure its length, elbow to wrist, and say I was going to be tall, but I couldn't count on that.

Patting his empty shirt pocket, Hans said, "I'm going up to the station for smokes. Want to ride along?"

I stood and stretched and yawned. Heidi stood and stretched and yawned, too, then followed us to the pickup and leaped straight into the air, landing in the bed of the truck and settling in her usual corner, her back against the cab right behind where I sat.

We coasted slow and easy up Mariposa Street, neither of us in any hurry to get to the station. The houses we passed stared back at us with blank window eyes, sheltering their dogs. There were two pit bulls on the corner, three Dobermans, two shepherds and four rottweilers, and a shepherd-wolf cross that was worse than any of them except maybe the pit bulls.

Heidi wasn't like those dogs behind their fences. I wasn't sure whether I was glad or not that she was quiet and intelligent instead of being a barking, snarling fool. Part of me loved her for it and felt like she was really my soul mate. The other part of me wanted a dog that everyone would be scared of—everyone but me.

Maybe I wanted to hide behind her. Maybe I wanted her to do my knife-fighting for me, when the time came. Who knows?

At the corner of Mariposa and Highway 47 was a Bronco Mart, combination gas station, grocery store, video arcade and liquor store. Its doors and windows were covered with metal security grids, like a jail, but it got robbed all the time anyway.

We stopped in front of the pumps, and I jumped out before Hans could beat me to the pump. I liked flipping the gas lever, jamming the nozzle into the tank, and watching the numbers tick around. Heidi stayed where she was, watching me. She hated the gas fumes.

"You stay there," I told her. She sank into lying-down position and rested her chin on the top of the truck-bed's side.

Through the window I could see old Jesse White Crow watching us with his binoculars. If people he didn't know drove up, he wouldn't turn on the pumps until they came in and paid for their gas, but he knew Hans and me.

"Ten bucks' worth," Hans yelled at me, and went inside. I stared at the spinning numbers on the pump and got into the rhythm, counting out loud. "Eight-fifty, sixty, seventy, eighty . . ." I had my rhythm just right when ten rolled up, and I cut it off just at the exact split second.

"You stay there," I told Heidi again, and went on inside.

"Hey, Jesse."

"How ya doing?" he greeted me.

Jesse wasn't really old, probably about thirty or forty.

We just called him old, I guess because he was so fat. He sat on a high stool behind his counter all day and never moved except to pick up his binoculars or to ring up a sale and make change.

"Ten even, on the gas," I told him. He peered through the binos at the figures on the pump, just to be sure. I said he knew us, I didn't say he trusted us. He didn't trust anyone. But I liked him anyway. He wore his black hair in a long braid down his back. It seemed dignified, to me.

Wandering down the aisle of candy and crackers and nacho chips made me want money of my own. Fourteen years old. Still too young for a real job. I opened the cooler at the back, took out a can of Coke, and popped the tab. Now Hans would have to buy it for me. I'd pay him back in a few years when I was old enough for a real job.

"Hey!" Jesse yelled. "You gotta pay for that before you open it, punk."

"Hans?" I said, begging.

Hans slapped down two quarters on top of the gas and cigarette money, but he gave me a killing look. I went over to the video games and said, "I'll play you for it, Hansie. Okay?"

"You already owe it to me—what you gonna play with, your shoelaces?"

But he came over anyway and fed more money into

the machine. Lights flashed, bells rang, and tiny, blocky tanks and planes began shooting each other. Hans got his score up to six hundred, then I took over. Two hundred, two-fifty . . .

At two-eighty I got blasted off the screen. We went another round, trying for best two out of three, but Hans beat me again, so we gave it up.

"So long, Jesse."

He lifted a hand but didn't look up from the copy of *Penthouse* that he kept under the counter at all times.

Outside, the heat came down on us and slowed our steps toward the pickup. Heidi's head was no longer resting on top of the side panel.

"Heidi? You asleep in there?"

I looked over the edge.

She was gone.

2

_____

"Oh no, oh no." The words echoed all through me as I ran. Up Mariposa and back to the station, up and down Forty-Seven I pounded, dreading to see a black body at the side of the road.

I shouldn't have left her that long in the back of the truck.

Hans moved the truck away from the pumps, and I yelled and called, behind the Bronco station and through the adjoining yards. No Heidi.

I stopped to catch my breath against the gas pump, and to listen. If Heidi was wandering loose in the neighborhood, the fenced dogs would be raising the roof, but I didn't hear any barking.

My throat began to close in an ache of needing to cry, but Hans was there, so I couldn't.

"Somebody stole her," he said.

I stared at him. "She could have left on her own," I said. But she never had. She wouldn't.

"Somebody stole her," he insisted. "They either

drove up and saw her and made off with her, or else they were walking past and just took her."

I knew he was right.

The station was getting busy now, with people going home from work.

Hans sighed and climbed into the truck, then motioned with his head for me to follow. "We can't just leave!" I wailed.

A car pulled up behind us and honked for us to move. Hans glared and made a threatening gesture, but drove out onto Mariposa anyway, coasting in slow motion up the street.

We drove around that block as slowly as we could, then around the next block, then back to the highway and up and down it for half an hour.

Finally Hans said, "We have to get home. It's supper time, and anyhow we're not going to find her this way. Somebody stole her, Sox. We could drive around till we dropped dead and we still wouldn't find her."

I did cry then. I couldn't help it. I turned my face toward the window and gulped against it but it came anyway. We were almost home by that time, so Hans drove around a couple more blocks to give me time to get hold of myself.

I hurt all over, inside and out, just like I'd been beaten. Heidi was gone, maybe forever. It was more than I could stand. It left a hole in my life so big I could fall down into it and disappear forever, myself. And it was my fault. I knew it was. I was the one who'd left her alone in the back of the truck. Never mind the fact that I'd been doing it for three years with no problem.

They were all in the kitchen when we went in: Dad and Ric at the table, Mama dishing up. Hans did the explaining; my voice wasn't dependable yet, from the crying. They all said just what I knew they would: Mama said, "Sit down and eat. We talk later." Dad said, "She'll show up." Ric's black eyes flashed and he half rose, ready for action. He swore so bad Mama had to shush him, and he started making bloody threats against whoever stole his little brother's dog.

I had to sit at the table and go through the motions of eating supper, but as soon as it was over I was ready to head out again, looking for Heidi.

"Just hold your horses," Dad said. He lumbered over to the phone on the kitchen wall and started dialing. "Let me talk to Juan," he said.

I steamed with impatience. Juan was one of the men who worked for Dad, doing lawn and pool maintenance up in the rich part of town. Why did he have to talk business when . . .

"Juan. Sorry to bother you at night. Heidi is lost or stolen, and we're going to go out looking for . . . Right. Thanks."

He made three more calls to the rest of his men and by the time he hung up, Juan was pulling up outside, ready to go.

I stood in the front yard listening to Dad and thinking he should be an army general or a big shot executive, the way he could organize people. Each one of his lawn-crew guys was assigned a section to search, Mariposa south to Broad, Forty-Seven to Riverside, and so on. Hans and Ric took one section, and Mama stayed home in case someone found Heidi and called. Our phone number was on Heidi's tags.

"What about me?" I said, finally. This was supposed to be my search, after all. She was my dog. Dad just looked down at me as if he'd forgotten me.

"I'll walk," I said. "Between here and Bronco Mart."

And so we went off in our assigned directions. Shadows stretched out long and thin as the sun got close to the horizon, and it wasn't quite as hot as it had been. My shadow led the way as I walked east up the broken sidewalks.

I called and called for Heidi, and I asked everyone I passed—the little kids skateboarding in the street and the few older people sitting out on porches. No one had seen a black German shepherd.

As I walked I tried to think logically. Heidi had to've been stolen. She wouldn't willingly leave the truck, I was sure of that. And even if she had jumped out, she'd have headed right for me, inside the store. Or she'd have been close around there when Hans and I came out.

I tried to picture someone walking along past the station, seeing Heidi, deciding to steal her. No, it didn't seem logical. Heidi held back from people till she had a chance to look them over. If I told her they were okay, she made up to them, but otherwise she'd hold back, looking them over. It would've taken several minutes for a stranger to coax her out of that truck and away from the station, and all that time they'd have been in plain sight of Jesse and Hans and me if we'd happened to look out.

But we didn't, did we? I argued. Hans and I were concentrating on the video game, Jesse was reading his girlie magazine.

So it was possible that it happened that way. Or . . . I tried to remember. Hadn't someone come in while we were at the video game? Hadn't someone come in and paid for gas and left again fast? Was that a possibility, then? Could that have been the one who took her?

Again I tried to picture it. This person, maybe two or three guys, drive in, pull up on the other side of the pump from Hans's truck. That would be the only place they could pull up to, with our truck there. Their car or truck would be between the station and our truck then, blocking the view of Heidi. They pull up there and start admiring Heidi while they're getting their gas. Then, while one of them comes into the station and pays, the other one lures Heidi, grabs her, keeps her from barking, stashes her away in their car, and they take off.

Yes. It was possible. Not very likely, but still it seemed at least as likely as anything else I could think of.

It was a starting point, anyway. If Jesse knew that guy . . .

I ran the last block to the Bronco and pulled open the door, puffing for breath. But it wasn't Jesse behind the counter, only the night lady, the one with the wrinkled neck and dyed red hair.

Jesse had told Hans once that he never worked the night shift himself because he had a theory that hoods would be less likely to rob a little old lady store clerk than they would an Indian. Hans and Ric and Jeraldo roared and hooted over that one. They all said Jesse was chicken, that's why he only worked days and made up that stupid theory. Sometimes I was scared stiff that those guys would find out how chicken I was. I couldn't stand to be laughed at like they laughed at Jesse.

"I've got to talk to Jesse," I said to the lady. "Do you know where he lives?"

She was reading Jesse's *Penthouse* magazine herself. I never knew ladies read those. "Down at Isleta," she said.

Isleta. The reservation. I couldn't get all the way to the reservation to look for Jesse. I'd have to wait till tomorrow.

I walked partway home, then Juan came along and picked me up. None of the searchers had found Heidi.

At seven the next morning I met Jesse unlocking the front door. I started throwing questions at him but he made me wait till he got the pumps turned on, the back door unlocked, and all the lights switched on in the cooler cases. Finally he settled his flabby body on his stool and looked at me.

I began my questions again with strained patience. "Yesterday afternoon when Hans and I were in here playing the video, who was it that came in and bought gas? I'm trying to find out if somebody stole my dog."

He'd been aware of the search yesterday, but he hadn't been any help. Now he stared at the ceiling, shook his head, shrugged. "Some guy, I didn't know him."

"What did he look like?"

He closed his eyes to ponder. "Nothing special. White guy, medium sized."

"Come on, Jesse, this is important. You have to remember more than that. Did he ever come in before? What was he wearing? What was he driving?"

Jesse yawned, showing me all his gold fillings. I wanted to beat him bloody.

"Wearing, let's see, T-shirt, I guess. White T-shirt, jeans. I think he had a beard or a mustache maybe. I don't remember what he was driving, kid."

I clenched my teeth. "Did you check the pump with your binos, Jesse?"

Again he pondered. "Yeah, I did. Yeah, I checked the pump with my eyes." He patted the black casing of the binos—his "eyes."

"Pickup, I think it was."

I held my breath. It was coming now, even if I had to pull it out one word at a time.

"What color, Jesse?"

"Red one. Or white. No, red truck, white thing on the back. Twelve bucks' worth of regular."

Regular gas. So it would be an old truck, probably. "What kind of white thing?"

"You know." Jesse made a shape with his hands.

"Like a camper, or a topper?" I urged.

"Yeah. Not a big high one. Kind of a low one it was. Little windows on the sides."

"Was there anyone else in the truck?"

He shook his head.

I started to leave, thinking Jesse was pumped dry. When I got to the door he said, "There was another guy, but not in the truck. He was over by yours, I think. Petting your dog."

3

I ran the six blocks home, charged with excitement.
Now I knew what had happened to Heidi—at least,
probably. My sadness and frustration were boiling up
into a rage that demanded action.

Mama was in the kitchen feeding the babies their
breakfasts. Not our babies, neighbor kids that Mama
took care of while their mothers worked. Sierra sat on
a pile of phone books to make her high enough, and
slapped at her cereal with the back of her spoon to
watch the milk drops fly. Marita was littler. She just
propped her fat arms against the high-chair tray and
opened her mouth automatically for each spoonload
of baby food Mama raised, never smiling, just staring
with her huge eyes and opening up like a baby bird.

Mama was like a bird herself. This year we were the
same height, but I could pick her up with no strain at
all. Sometimes I came up behind her and raised her
off her feet and held her there till she yelled and
swatted me. I could get my fingers around her wrists,
easy. She wore her hair in a single braid, like Jesse

White Crow, and it made her look young until you saw the lines in her face. Then you could tell she'd been taking care of kids for a long time—her own and other people's. We all wore her out, I guess.

Sometimes I didn't understand why people had babies in the first place. Like now, with all the mess of feeding these two. But when I thought about how good it felt to be in a family, with lots of people to help you when you needed it, it made more sense. You had to go through the baby part of it in order to get the family part of it.

And right now was sure one of those times when I needed that family.

Ric had worked full-time for Dad since he got out of school, and the two of them were long gone. In hot weather they generally worked from six in the morning till about noon, sat around in cool bars all afternoon or came home and slept, then worked another four or five hours in the evening. Hans had a summer job on a road construction crew, so he was gone already, too.

That left just Mama. She made me eat some breakfast while I told her about the two men in the red-and-white pickup camper. "I'm going to find those guys and get Heidi back," I finished savagely.

Mama gave me a cool look while she guided Marita's orange-juice bottle toward the open mouth. That dumb baby would drink forever, but she wouldn't hold the bottle herself. Mama had to prop her elbow on the high-chair tray and hold the stupid bottle the whole time.

Sierra started her usual whimpering that meant she was through eating. I mopped off her face with her bib and lifted her down from the stack of telephone books.

"Bugs," she demanded, dancing and pulling at my hand. She hauled me to the TV in the living room and sat down right in front of it while I turned on her "Bugs Bunny" cartoon show. She knew she'd get her hand smacked if she touched the TV herself.

Back in the kitchen I said, "Mama, should I tell the police, do you think?"

She concentrated on the baby so she wouldn't have to look at me. Mama had a huge fear of the police. I knew it from the way she looked and acted when anyone talked about them. Hans told me once that it was because Mama's parents came up from Mexico illegally in the trunk of an old car. They never got deported, and Mama was born a legal citizen, but I guess she caught her fear from them. Mama was the most honest person I ever knew, but she was still scared silly of policemen or anyone like them. Maybe that was why she refused to learn to drive: fear of being stopped for a ticket.

But she knew, and I knew, the logical thing to do was to call the police. We had to at least report Heidi stolen. Anything that would raise the odds of getting her back, we had to do.

"I'll call the police myself, okay?" I offered.

Mama cleaned Marita off and set her on the floor, and said without looking at me, "No, I'll call. They won't take a kid seriously. I'll call them."

"Now?"

She sighed. I could see the effort it took for her to open the phone book that was still on the stack on Sierra's chair, to find the page of emergency numbers, to say the number over and over to herself, and then to pick up the phone and dial it.

I got my ear up beside hers, where I could hear.

"Police station."

"Hello? Yes, please, could I talk to someone? Our dog is stolen?"

She was sweating with fear, and all her sentences came out sounding like questions. I wished I'd made the call myself, even if they wouldn't take me as seriously as her.

"One moment, I'll transfer you." And then another voice. "Robbery."

"Hello, yes? This is Mrs. George Newmann, 1542 Mariposa Lane, Albuquerque."

"Yes?"

"Our dog got stolen." Her voice grew more normal as she described Heidi, and the where and when of the robbery, and the two men in the red pickup camper.

"A German shepherd, you say." The man's voice was businesslike, but nice. "We've had some other dog thefts in your end of town, ma'am, and we're investigating. Thank you for your call. We'll sure let you know if we find anything."

I turned the phone toward my own face and said, "Sir? This is Sox Newmann. She's my dog. Do you think she's okay? Do you think you can track down the pickup, and find her? Is she still alive, do you think?" All my worst thoughts spilled out between my words.

He understood. "I can't say, son. Probably. The dogs that are disappearing are all watchdog-type breeds, so we're figuring they may be going out of state for resale as guard dogs, or something like that. I know how much you want her back. I've got a Brittany myself and I know how I'd feel. But at least I don't think you need to worry about her being harmed. She'd be too valuable. I know that's not much comfort. . . ."

We hung up the phone and Mama gave me a long, hard hug that told me how much she was hurting for me. During the hug I noticed that Heidi's food dish wasn't in the corner by the refrigerator.

She didn't have a water dish because she preferred to drink out of the toilet. I tried to break her of the habit, but even if you left the lid down she'd shove it up with her nose and get her head in there anyway, and then leave a trail of wet across the seat after she drank. Finally we just started leaving the seat up, too, and her water bowl went back to being a mixing bowl.

I walked through the house: four small, square rooms full of familiar smells and clutter, kitchen and living room across the front, two bedrooms at the back with bathroom between. Even with Luther and Cruzi both married and moved away it's still crowded. There were clothes and baby toys and diapers in all the usual places, but no rawhide bone under the end table. No shoe sole, knotted sock or eyeless stuffed bear on or under my bed. Heidi's and my bed.

Mama had put Heidi's stuff away this morning while I was at the station. She didn't think Heidi was coming back, and she didn't want me having to look at the bear, and the sock, and the other stuff.

I got out of the house fast and did my bawling in the garage.

Without thinking much about what I was doing, I untangled the two rusty old bikes, saw which one had air in the tires, and pumped off down the street on it. I'd quit riding bikes this past year because I wanted so badly to be driving a car. The bikes just seemed too young for me, even though I still had a year and seven months to go before driving age.

But today I had to get away from that dogless house. I had to be doing something to try to find Heidi, even something as useless as riding around looking for red pickups. There was so much mad in me, I didn't even feel the work of pedaling. I wanted to kill those guys. I just wanted to track them down, and get my hands on them, and kill them.

Any time the mad thoughts died down, worse ones took their place: thoughts about where Heidi was at that moment. Was she in some hot place without water or food? Was she as scared and mad and frantic as I was, being separated from her? Were they beating her or hurting her or yelling at her?

I couldn't stand thinking about it.

And I couldn't stand thinking how many of Jesse's customers are just passing through town on Forty-Seven, heading south toward the border, or north, or anywhere, and just happen to pull in there for gas. There was a good chance Heidi was in Old Mexico or Arizona or Colorado or Texas by now. Or even farther, if they drove all night.

I was going north along the highway now, sitting back on the seat instead of hunching over the bars. My eyes scanned the highway and every side street, looking for a red pickup with a white topper.

One thing gave me hope. The cop had said that other dogs in the area were being stolen—all of them guard dog breeds. If somebody around here was swiping watchdogs, and if they were the ones who got Heidi, then she wasn't hundreds of miles away.

Yet.

But she might be if I didn't find her pretty soon. The cop said they were probably swiping the dogs to sell out of town, and that made sense. Sell a stolen dog too close to home and someday the old owner and the new owner are going to make contact, and your butt will be in a sling.

So, time was important. I had to find her fast.

4

Every morning, right after breakfast, I called the animal shelter to see if a black German shepherd had been picked up. At first the people were patient and sympathetic with me, but after a while they started getting a little hard-voiced, telling me they *had* my name and phone number and if they got a black German shepherd they would call me. So I quit bugging them and concentrated on the search.

It was on the afternoon of my third day of bike patrolling that I found the truck.

I'd been systematically covering every street, north-south and east-west, for forty blocks around the Bronco Mart. When I finished that, the evening of the second day, I started over again—but this time just patrolling the main streets, Highway Forty-Seven and two east-west ones.

Several times I caught sight of red pickups, but not with white toppers on the back. One did have a white camper and I pedaled like crazy to catch up with it at a stop sign. But it was a big high camper with bed space over the truck's cab. It was plastered with bumper stickers from the Grand Canyon, Mammoth Cave, and the Continental Divide, and it was an old guy driving with his wife.

And then he was there. He was just there, a foot away from me.

I was at the stop sign waiting to get onto Forty-Seven, and since I had to turn left, I needed a break in the traffic. It was five-thirty, just when everybody was pouring south down Forty-Seven, going home from work. I'd bent over to look at the bike's chain because it was starting to slip sometimes when I came down on a pedal with all my weight.

Something pulled up beside me, something red. I straightened up and glanced, not expecting the jackpot. I'd had three straight days of disappointments by then.

Red pickup, an old one with fenders ragged at the edges, and paint turning to rust. Dirty white topper on the back with a small window so close I could touch it if I reached out. The window had material stretched over it on the inside, not hanging in folds like a curtain, but stretched tight like it was nailed in place.

I sat there balanced on one foot, just staring. The numbness of surprise only lasted a second, but then I dithered another second trying to decide what to do. I pushed forward a few feet and stared in through the darkened cab window. Only one person inside, a white guy with a little bit of scraggly beard and hair that looked dark blond or light brown. Middle-sized guy, maybe thirty. Just like Jesse said.

He'd been looking left, away from me, and watching for a traffic break like I'd been doing. But while I stared, thinking, "This is him. He's got Heidi," his face turned in my direction, his eyes still on the traffic.

I couldn't stop staring at him. I couldn't move to do any of the things I should be doing. He felt my eyes, and met them with a look that started out blank but then grew curious. I could see him trying to figure out why that kid was staring at him.

Finally my mind went into gear. I started backing my bike toward the rear of the truck. But before I could read the license plate the truck roared forward in a cloud of dark exhaust smoke and swung left onto the highway.

The license plate went by so fast that its numbers and letters blurred and disappeared before I could get my eyes in gear to read them. I had an impression of three letters, a space, and three numbers, and one of the letters might have been a *C*, but that was all I got.

On TV people can always read the whole license plate in a millionth of a second from a block away. Not in real life, I told myself furiously. All that time

I wasted staring at the guy I could have spent memorizing the darn number.

The traffic gap closed as soon as the truck got through it, so I bumped my bike up onto the sidewalk and pedaled harder than I'd ever pedaled in my life.

"Get off the sidewalk!" an old lady yelled after me as I skimmed past her and her shopping cart. The white topper was still in sight, but it was two blocks ahead of me and gaining.

Another break in the traffic. I banged down over the curb and went like hell up the middle of the highway, straining to see that white topper. But now the sun was turning the tops of all the cars into a colorless glare of reflected sun. My eyes started watering from the effort of staring south into the sun.

The truck disappeared in the glare and the traffic, but I kept after it anyway, looking up each side street I passed. On and on I pedaled, too mad to give up: mad at the crook who stole my best friend, mad at myself for blowing it at the stop sign.

Finally I had to turn and start the endless trip home. I'd gone a good two miles farther south than I'd been before, and for a while it didn't look like I would ever see that Bronco Mart sign that meant Mariposa and home.

It was nine o'clock and just about dark when I finally dumped the bike in the garage and went inside. But

Dad and Ric had just got there, too, so I ate my supper with them. Most work days in summer we had late suppers anyhow. Hans was out on a date, but I told the rest of them about seeing the truck.

They didn't seem very excited. Ric said it probably wasn't the same guy that was at the Bronco when Heidi got swiped, and Dad just sort of grunted and went on eating. Heidi was four days gone now, and I knew Dad had written her off. He probably figured it didn't hurt anything if I wanted to go looking for her, at least for a few days just to give me something to do, to help me get over losing her. But by now I could tell from his face and what he didn't say that he thought it was time for me to give up and forget about her.

Dad never had a dog, not when he was a kid—not ever, till we got Heidi. He didn't know what it felt like, losing her. To him she was just a big animal that knocked things off the coffee table when she wagged her tail, and got dirt and dog hairs on my bed sheets, sleeping with me.

He didn't have a clue how it felt to roll over in the night and feel Heidi stretched out beside me, strong and brave and loyal even when she was sleeping. How it felt when she brought that ratty stuffed bear and tossed it on my stomach when I was lying on the floor watching television, how her eyes would sparkle at me till I played her game with her. I'd hide the bear under my body and pretend it wasn't there until she pawed it out and raced away with it.

If I'd roll over on my stomach on the floor and hide my face in my arms and pretend to cry, Heidi would go crazy, whining and jabbing her face toward mine, under my arms. Then I'd turn the pretend crying into laughing, and roll over and grab her and wrestle with her, and she'd get all charged up with silliness. She knew all along I wasn't crying. It was just our game.

Dad never understood any of that, just the dirt she brought in and the cost of dog food.

So it was Ric I aimed at when I said, "I can't do it on my bike, Ric. That guy is here in this area, and he's bound to show up again somewhere along Forty-Seven, but I can't follow him on a bike. Would you help me?"

He and Dad exchanged a look.

"Will you?" I demanded. "On your afternoon break? Tomorrow? If I don't find her pretty soon it's going to be too late."

Dad looked down at his plate and went on chewing. He had a round face with round features, but it was still a hard face. It didn't smile much, and it was hard to read when he closed it up like this.

Ric said, "Maybe. We'll see how our time goes. We've got to take a pool filter apart, up by Los Ranchos. It's kicking sand out through the intakes, so we might have to replace some laterals. If we get done in time . . ."

I looked from him to Dad, and I knew they wouldn't show up tomorrow or any other time. They'd talked about me already, about this hunt I was on, and Dad had said, "Best not to encourage him. He's never going to find her. Time to forget the dog and let life get back to normal."

After supper I went to bed and lay there in the dark, trying to think what to do next. My bed was a low narrow one against the wall by the window. Ric and Hans had the big one that took up most of the rest of the room. I lay on my side with my head at the foot end of the bed, where I could prop up on an elbow and stare out the window. There was nothing out there to look at, but I always thought better if I could look far away.

Lately I'd started collecting wisdom, or trying to. I never told any of the guys I ran around with or they'd have made fun of me, but I did it anyway. I was trying to build Sox Newmann into the smartest person I could, not book-smart but the kind of smart, or wise, that gets you through life with the fewest hurts and problems.

In school we had to memorize a poem called "If," by Rudyard Kipling. I never thought I'd like a poem but I liked that one because it seemed to have wise answers for any problem that could come up in life.

That poem didn't help with this situation, but something else I heard or read came back to me as I stared out that window. To beat your enemy, think like he does and then think past him.

So, okay. I was a dog thief. I drove around in a pickup with an enclosed back end, looking for watchdog-type dogs that could be snatched. Then I took them . . . somewhere safe where people wouldn't see me bringing them in. Then I'd sell them someplace far away from Albuquerque so their former owners wouldn't accidentally run into them at the vet's or the shopping mall parking lot.

Right. So how do I get my customers? Who buys the dogs? Maybe a partner in some other state. Or maybe I sell them directly to the new owners. That would make more profit than splitting with a partner.

If I were wanting to sell guard dogs, where and how would I do it?

I squeezed my eyes shut and concentrated. Uncle Luis. Uncle Luis bred Heidi's mother once or twice every year, and raised six or eight pups each time. He sold them from ads in the Albuquerque Sunday paper.

Ads in the Sunday paper.

5

When I was in sixth grade we had a library class where we learned how to look stuff up in the library and find out anything we needed to know. For once I could see a reason for all that studying and learning. Now I needed information badly, and I knew where to get it.

I spent the morning pedaling over to the South Albuquerque branch library and looking up addresses. First I studied the U.S. map in the atlas and picked out twenty cities that I'd put ads in if I was the dog thief. Then I got the phone directories for all those cities and got the names and addresses of their main newspapers.

It took most of the afternoon to write the twenty letters. The hard part was figuring out what to say. I ended up just saying the truth, that my dog got stolen and I was trying to find her, and did their paper have any ads for watchdogs for sale from someone in Albuquerque.

One of Mama's babies was cutting a tooth and kept

whining and crying, and that didn't help my concentration. Mama was tired and crabby herself, from the baby's noise, so I didn't ask her to help, but I did have to ask for paper and envelopes, and for five dollars for stamps. I told her I was writing letters that might help find Heidi, and she gave me what I needed. But she also gave me a long sad look, like she was telling me it wasn't going to work, don't get my hopes up.

I knew that. But I had to try.

I took the letters all the way up to South Albuquerque Post Office, twenty blocks away. After I'd dropped them through the slot, I rode down Forty-Seven to the corner where I'd seen my red truck yesterday. I sat for an hour, waiting and watching, just in case he came by there every day at the same time, maybe on his way home from work or something. But he didn't come.

All the rest of that week I truck-hunted, sometimes catching a distant glimpse of my truck or one like it, but never close enough to go after it.

At night I'd lie on my bed staring out the window and thinking about those twenty letters going off in all directions.

Every day that went past made me feel more hopeless. If Heidi was stolen by professional dog thieves she was probably gone by now. If I could find the thieves, there was a bare possibility I could track Heidi through them, if they kept records of their sales. But it wasn't a very big hope and it got smaller every day.

The other possibility was that whoever took Heidi wanted her for themselves. In that case I might not ever get her back.

The guys I run around with got tired of me. They thought I was *loco en la cabeza,* spending two weeks chasing a long-gone dog. Well, maybe I was crazy in the head. But I had to keep on doing it anyway. Heidi meant more to me than all those guys put together. I mean, they were my buddies. We went to school together and hung around together and talked about football and sex and stuff like that. But there wasn't one of them who would have risked his own safety to protect me if I was in trouble.

Heidi would. I knew she would. She loved me more than anyone in the world. Well, except my family of course, but Heidi worshipped me. Just me. I was the most important thing in her life, and you don't get that from a bunch of guys who just hang out together.

So by the second week of my bike hunt, those guys had quit coming around. They waved at me if I went past them, but nothing more.

And then, on Tuesday of that second week, two letters came, addressed to me. They were in business-sized envelopes with printed return addresses, from the *Phoenix Arizona Republic* and the *El Paso Herald Post.*

I was holding my breath so hard I could barely get the envelopes open. "Please, God. Please, God," I prayed as I pulled out the first letter:

Dear Mr. Newmann,

In reply to your letter I am enclosing a clipping from our classified department. I hope this will be of some help.

And a signature I didn't bother to read.
Taped to the letter was an ad that read:

Trained guard dogs for sale. Protect your home, your family, your business. Attack-trained Rotts, Dobes, Shepherds, and Malamutes. $1,000 to $3,000. Guardian Angel Kennels, Box 361, Albuquerque, NM.

This was it.

Hope flared like a torch as I read the ad over and over. The second letter was like the first, and enclosed the same ad. I was disappointed that the ads didn't list an address, but then I guessed the crooks would want to keep as hidden as they could and still get letters from people wanting to buy their dogs.

All I had to do now was call the post office, find out the address of Box 361, and go there. Heidi was probably still there, getting trained. If they were selling trained dogs, then it would take a while to train them, a month or two at the very least. I could go there with a policeman, maybe, or at least with Dad and Ric and Hans, and just get Heidi back.

I ran in the house and tried to tell Mama, but she was rocking Marita and massaging her gums while Marita whimpered and fussed, so I don't think Mama really heard what I was saying.

I grabbed the phone book and looked up Guardian Angel Kennels. It wasn't listed in the white pages or the yellow pages. When I called the post office and asked about Box 361, they said they couldn't give out that information.

"Please," I begged. "They stole my dog and I have to find her before they sell her someplace far away."

The man I was talking to passed me on to his boss who listened to my story. "I'm sorry," he said. "I'd help if I could, but we absolutely cannot give out that information. All I can tell you is that the three-hundred box numbers are from the south branch. And I shouldn't tell you that much. But I used to have a dog—he was half shepherd, I think. He got stolen, too. Good luck, kid. Wish I could be more help, but I'd lose my job, you know?"

I thanked him politely, but I couldn't help slamming the phone when I hung up. That man had the key. He knew where Guardian Angel Kennels was, where

Heidi was. Even though I understood about him losing his job, I couldn't help wanting to strangle him and get the address out of him.

Still, he did say one valuable thing. Box 361 was at the South Albuquerque Post Office. That's where my red truck would have to come every day to pick up the mail.

It wasn't much, but it was a starting point.

The post office opened at eight. I was there the next morning when they unlocked the door. I parked my bike under a shade tree at the back of the parking lot and settled in to watch and wait.

The time dragged past. I couldn't believe how long it took for the first hour to go by. The second one took even longer.

Maybe the guy doesn't pick up his mail every day, I thought. Or maybe somebody else picks it up for him, in a different car. Or maybe my red truck isn't connected with Box 361 at all, and the two guys at the Bronco station didn't take Heidi after all. Or . . .

There he was.

The red pickup came out of nowhere and coasted into one of the ten-minute parking spaces in front of the post office. I'd been watching so hard I almost didn't realize it was him.

But it was. I knew it. It was the same truck I'd seen

at the stop sign, with the curtain material nailed across the windows of the white topper.

I was shaking all over as I picked up my bike and got into position behind a parked car so I could follow the pickup when it pulled away from the curb. I couldn't get close enough to read the license plate without being seen.

The guy came out right away and walked toward the truck. He was the same one I'd seen before, with the light brown hair and skimpy beard. I crouched down so I was looking at him through car windows but he couldn't see me. He'd gotten a good look at me once before, at the stop sign when we stared at each other; I didn't want him to see me again and start thinking I was following him.

The truck started up, pulled away, then turned a hard right and came through the parking lot, toward my hiding place. I panicked and pedaled away, head still down.

He roared past me and out into the street again without seeming to notice me. I realized then that he'd only driven through the parking lot to turn around and head back down the street the same way he'd come, from the south.

I pedaled like crazy and managed to stay with him for six blocks before I lost him.

"Okay," I thought grimly as I headed home. "Today wasn't payoff day, but I got closer. I know what time he picks up his mail, and I know part of the way he comes.

"I'll get him yet. I'll follow him home if it takes all summer."

I knew then that it wasn't only Heidi I wanted. It was revenge, too.

6

My red truck had been at the post office a little after ten that morning. The next day I was in position by nine, not at the post office this time, but along Forty-Seven at the point where I'd lost sight of him yesterday.

I sat in front of an office supply store, in the shade of their awning, and stared south down the highway watching for him. The guy in the office supply store started giving me dirty looks through the window after a while, but I sat there anyhow.

About ten-thirty the truck came swimming along out of the shimmery waves of heat that rose from the highway. He went north past me, heading for the post office.

I took off south, covered the three or four blocks to the point where I first saw him, and parked again. This time there was no shade. Along this stretch were small ratty-looking businesses mixed in with small ratty-looking houses.

I sat beside a parked car and strained to look north over my shoulder. As soon as I saw the truck I pushed off, keeping on the sidewalk. I'd gained almost a block by the time the truck roared past. He needed a new muffler, bad.

I went into high gear and pumped as hard as I could. We gained almost twelve blocks before I lost him again in the traffic and the glare and shimmer of the sun. Rio Bravo Boulevard. I memorized where I was, and headed home.

Next day I left home earlier and got to Rio Bravo by nine. My truck went past just a few minutes later, but this time it took longer for him to get to the post office and back to me, and I was six blocks south of Rio Bravo when he roared past. Again I followed him as fast and as far as I could.

By now we were getting out of the city. Houses were farther apart and farther back from the highway, but they were still small ratty-looking places. Some of them had rusty wire mesh fences, with chickens and goats in the yards.

I waited three blocks south of the last sighting the next morning, figuring I could pick up a few free blocks that way. I teetered on my bike in a shady spot under a store awning just up a side street from the highway corner. My truck went past, right on schedule. When the time came for it to be coming back south, I eased up closer to the corner, ready to whip out after him as soon as he went past.

He never came. I waited four more hours, and he never came. But on the following morning he appeared, going north, just when he was supposed to, and came back south when I expected him, and I gained another twenty blocks before I lost him.

The next day, I went several blocks beyond where I'd last seen the truck, and waited there. He didn't come. I waited all day till the post office was closed, but he didn't come. Either his route turned somewhere north of where I waited, in that several-block area where I hadn't actually seen him, or else he just didn't make the mail-run that day.

The next morning, I backed up to the corner where I had definitely seen the truck two days before. He came at nine-thirty, but he came from a side street, turning north onto Forty-Seven a block south of where I sat.

"That was it. That was my mistake yesterday," I thought with a savage kind of satisfaction.

After he went past, I rode to his corner and went two blocks east and waited again, this time behind a clump of sick-looking cactus in somebody's yard. The cactus was higher than my head, and full of big rotten holes where birds or something had been eating on it. I felt sorry for it.

This street was wider than most of the residential streets around, but it looked older and more beat-up. The pavement was all broken and patched, and the houses were littler and crummier than up where I lived, which wasn't any Beverly Hills.

I saw the truck as soon as it turned off the highway, two blocks behind me. I was in full gear and pedaling fast by the time he passed me up.

"Does he recognize me yet?" I wondered. I'd been wearing different clothes each day just in case, white T-shirt and jeans one day, red and black tank top and shorts the next day, and so on. I figured my bike looked like every other rusty old kid's bike in town, and I looked a little different each day because of the clothes, so maybe he wasn't noticing that the same kid was following him every day. Today I had on some old tan jeans of Hans's, cut off at the knees, and no shirt, and a baseball cap pulled down over my forehead.

Now that we were off the highway I could keep up with him pretty well. He had to go thirty instead of the fifty he'd been doing on the highway, because for one thing the street was so bad. He'd have broken something for sure, on that old truck, hitting these potholes any faster.

He was about a block ahead of me when he turned

left through a gate in a crooked, old, eight-foot-tall chain-link fence.

I slowed down, my heart thumping in my throat.

As soon as I realized it was a driveway, I stopped the bike and sat there, staring and thinking.

It was the last building on the street. Beyond it, the cracked old road led onto what looked like an abandoned airport of some kind, to the north and east. The regular Albuquerque airport was way north of where we were, so I knew this was something else. I could see three humpbacked hangars with faded letters painted over them: WALTER'S FLYING SERVICE.

The rest of the place was bare rocky dirt, weeds, and cracked runways, with cactus and sage taking over the land again.

I turned my attention to the building my truck had gone behind. It was a square, two-story cement block building with glass-block windows that you couldn't see through. It looked like some kind of factory or warehouse. Faded turquoise paint was peeling off the cement walls, and the weeds were just about up to the windows.

Then I heard something that made me stop thinking and just freeze.

Dogs barking.

Lots of dogs. Inside the building. Barking their

heads off. A man's voice bellowed out, and the barking stopped. But then I heard something worse. A scream, or a cry or howl of pain. I couldn't tell if it was animal or human, but it was terrible.

Time to get help, I thought. But first, the license plate number. I'd caught glimpses of it the past few days, but still not enough, not the whole thing. I'd been too busy watching where I was going. UCV was all I had.

I left my bike and went past the building, down the road toward the abandoned hangars. There was no one outside the dog building, and no windows except the glass-block ones, so I was fairly safe. Still, I kept down and circled toward the back of the building, keeping a screen of weeds and cactuses between me and it.

The truck was parked behind the building, beside what looked like a loading dock. There were big doors over the wooden dock, like trucks would back up to the dock and unload big stuff, and it would get hauled back inside, through the big doors.

I'd expected to see some dog pens in the back, but there weren't any. Whatever dogs were kept at Guardian Angel Kennels never saw the light of day, that was for sure.

I had to get almost up to the fence that separated the airport from the dog-warehouse place before I could read the license plate number through the chain links of the fence.

UCV 895.

I recited it over and over while I scooted back to my bike and rode home. UCV 895. I would never forget that number till the day I died, it was carved in my mind so deep by the time I got home.

I told Mama as soon as I got there, and begged her to call the police station. "No, you call them," she said. "You can tell them what you found out. They'll take care of it from there."

So I looked up the police number again, and dialed it and eventually got the same nice guy I'd talked to before. He listened to my whole story, and then he shot me down.

"I'll check on the license number for you," he said, "but don't count on it proving anything."

"But can't you go out there and see if they've got Heidi there?" I wailed.

"Not without a warrant, son. And I don't have enough to go on here, to swear out a warrant. You don't know that your dog was stolen by the two men you saw at the gas station. He might have been, but that's only a guess."

"*She!*" I yelled.

"She. And there's nothing substantial to connect the gas station people with this truck you've been following.

Red pickups with white toppers aren't all that rare. And you don't know for sure that the man you followed was connected with Box 361. He might have been, or he might not. And dogs barking inside a warehouse . . . you see what I mean? None of it adds up to enough to get a search warrant, much as I'd like to. I have a dog myself, and I'd like to get these guys, believe me. But you have to face facts. I've got three murders, two rapes and half a dozen burglaries with guns, not near enough men to handle even the murders, so you can see . . ."

I thanked him and hung up. Sure, I could see. Everybody was too busy to do anything to help. Maybe Dad or Hans, though.

They all got home about eight-thirty, and I told them everything I'd been doing and learning, while we ate supper.

Dad said, "You've been getting in over your head, Sox. These might be dangerous guys you're messing with. Best to leave it alone and let the police take care of it."

But Hans and Ric were on my side. I could see it in their faces. They were ready to fight for me. Heck, they loved to fight—I was just giving them an excuse.

We went to our room after supper and hunched together on the big bed.

"Tomorrow afternoon," Ric promised. "I'll leave

Dad in some nice cool bar with his nose in a mug of foamy beer, and we'll go out to that place." Then he asked Hans, "Can you get away?"

Hans nodded. "We're laying blacktop now, and we knock off around two because it gets too hot to pour till the sun starts going down. I won't have any trouble getting away for a couple of hours. Pick me up at the Git-n-Go, corner of Halston and Ninety-third." To me he said, "We'll pick you up at the Bronco, a little after two."

I lay awake most of the night, tense as a guitar string, thinking about maybe, tomorrow, getting Heidi back.

7

_____

"There it is," I said, pointing through the truck's windshield at the old warehouse. We coasted to a stop by the curb, then suddenly Hans pulled the pickup around in a tight circle, so that we were parked facing away from the dead end of the street.

"You never know," he muttered. "We might need to get out of here fast."

"Let's go," I said, and elbowed Ric towards the door. They always made me sit in the middle of the truck seat when we went anywhere.

"Not you." Hans's voice was hard. I froze and stared at him.

"No. Now listen," Hans said. "We're not going to barge in there and put them on their guard. Ric and I will go up there, tell them we're looking for a German shepherd to use as a watchdog. Tell them the guy at the liquor store down there on the corner told us that some guys up here had dogs to sell. See what they say."

"But I want to go," I wailed. "She's my dog. I should—"

"You're not going," Ric said. "It could be dangerous, and we're not taking you in there, so just shut up about it."

"But—"

Hans said, "Besides, we need you to stay out here and keep the motor running in case we get into trouble. And if we're not out in, say, half an hour, you go get help, okay?"

"Half an hour?" It sounded like an awfully long time.

"They may have some dogs to show us," Hans explained. "And if Heidi's in there, we'll have to get her away from them some way."

"We'll break their faces," Ric growled.

"Not unless we have to," Hans said, in a warning voice. I could tell they'd talked all this out before they picked me up at the Bronco station. It made me a little bit mad. This was supposed to be *my* rescue mission.

But when they slammed the truck doors and walked away through the weeds towards the back of the warehouse, I felt a shameful wash of relief. I hated thinking that I might be the kind of guy who hid behind his big brothers and let other people do his fighting for him.

I was willing to go in, I argued to myself. I wanted to go in. They wouldn't let me.

But the deeper, more honest part of me said, Oh yeah? How hard did you try? You should have gone anyway. You should have just gone.

I slid into the driver's seat and gunned the motor, turning the steering wheel in little jerky movements like a little kid pretending to drive. That's all I was, a little kid pretending to drive. Hiding behind his big brothers.

Then I forgot my own rotten self and concentrated on staring at the corner of the warehouse, where Heidi might be coming any second.

Suddenly they were there. Hans and Ric. No dog. They walked at an easy pace and showed no signs of a fight. My heart went all the way down to my shoes.

Heidi wasn't there. I fought back the tears so they wouldn't see.

They climbed in around me, slammed the doors, and we peeled away.

"She's not there," Hans said simply. "There was a guy in there, he acted friendly enough. We told him we were looking to buy us a watchdog, a shepherd."

"Yeah?" I prodded.

"Guy said he didn't have any shepherds. We said, could we take a look at the dogs he did have. He was kind of reluctant at first, but ol' Ric here flashed a wad . . ."

Ric patted his buttoned shirt pocket where I could see the shape of folded money. Ric loved money. He loved just touching it. He'd cash his paychecks and just carry the money till he'd spent it all.

". . . And then the guy showed us his dogs," Hans went on. "There was a bunch of 'em back there in pens, one that looked like it might be half shepherd, and the guy tried to sell us that one. But that was it. No Heidi."

Again I wanted to bawl, I was so disappointed. For the first time, I began to believe that Heidi was really truly gone for good. And if they'd already sold her, that meant they had her trained already, just in that short a time. My good, gentle Heidi, already turned into an attack dog. I couldn't stand to think about what they'd have had to do to her, to turn her mean that fast.

I couldn't stand the thought.

"What did the guy look like?" I asked.

Ric said, "You know Jesse White Crow?"

Hans sputtered and I grinned in spite of myself. Ric did this all the time.

"Okay," I said. "Yes, I know Jesse White Crow."

"Okay, you take Jesse White Crow, you cut off about a foot of height, shave off his hair, make him bald with a fringe of white hair around the edges, pink skin, little blue eyes, take away about a hundred pounds, a pot belly and a high squeaky voice, and you got the guy."

We needed the relief of laughing. I punched Ric in the arm and said, "He looks just like Jesse, except for Jesse being a three-hundred-pound, six-foot-tall Pueblo Indian with hair down to his waist. Right?"

"Right," Ric said placidly.

But I thought about the description. It sure wasn't my red pickup truck man. "Was there a truck parked back there? A red pickup, the one I was following?"

Hans and Ric shook their heads. "No truck, no nothing."

I mentally added that little piece to the puzzle. This short bald guy must either live within walking distance of the warehouse, or for some other reason not have a car there. That didn't tell me anything.

They dropped me off at home and left again to get back to their jobs. I sat on the back steps, away from the noise of the little kids' cartoon shows on television. There was serious thinking to be done.

Was I going to give in, start forgetting about Heidi now? Or was I going to keep on with it somehow?

Keep on, of course. I had to. Heidi was my partner, my buddy. I couldn't give her up without trying everything.

"I'll go out there myself. I'll see if they'll hire me for the summer, taking care of the dogs or something. Then maybe I'll be able to find out if they did steal Heidi, and possibly I could find out who they sold her to."

All that afternoon and evening, and far into the night, I planned my approach. I'd go out to the warehouse in the morning, after Red Truck Man had left for the post office, so I'd only have to talk to one guy, the little bald one. I'd tell him . . . I'd tell him I loved dogs and was looking for a summer job working with dogs, taking care of them and maybe learning to train them. I'd say that my two brothers had been out there looking to buy a shepherd, and had come home and told me about the place, so I thought I'd see if I could get a summer job there.

I tested the story over and over in my mind and the logic of it held up. Finally I went to sleep, but woke in the middle of the night. A thought had come up from the bottom part of my mind and shaken me awake.

Any men who steal dogs and sell them illegally probably aren't dog-lovers. Probably, they even mistreat the dogs while they have them, or at least get pretty rough with them. They're not going to want a kid hanging around who is a dog-lover. That kind of kid would get all upset about the way they treat their dogs, he might go home and tell somebody, and cause all kinds of trouble.

No. I couldn't go as a dog-lover. I'd have to pretend to be the same kind of person they are, if I was going to have any chance at all of them hiring me.

Another thought came in the quiet blackness of the night. These men probably wouldn't want a kid around under *any* circumstances, if they were doing something illegal. They probably wouldn't actually need any kennel help—none they'd have to pay for, anyhow. It might help if I offered to work free. But then I'd have to have a convincingly strong reason for wanting to work for them. No kid would want to work all summer and not get paid for it.

I couldn't think of anything I could say to those men that would make them want to have me around the place. Through the long night hours I lay awake, still not sure how I was going to do what I had to do.

8

It was a little after nine when I turned my bike into the dead-end street and pumped slowly toward the warehouse. Red Truck Man had passed me five minutes before, heading north toward the post office.

I leaned my bike against the flaking-paint concrete block wall of the warehouse and walked around the corner toward the back door, wondering how I was going to pull this off.

The only people-sized door was a windowless black steel one on a landing up several steps. The landing ran all along the side of the building, past huge truck-sized doors, to become what looked like a loading dock.

I banged on the door but didn't make much noise. It was enough, though, to start a million dogs barking inside the building. In a minute the door was pushed open a few inches. In the shadows beyond, I could see a round pale face no higher than my own. Bald head, tiny mouth, button nose.

"Hi," I said. "Are you the boss here?"

"Who wants to know?" the man said. Not a warm welcome. His voice was high-pitched and soft, more feminine than my sister Cruzi's even when she was trying to soften hers.

"Uh, my name is Sox Newmann. Could I come in a minute?" I'd decided to use my real name in case they did hire me, and paid me with checks. I wanted to be able to cash them.

"What do you want? I'm busy."

"Um, it'll only take a minute, okay? I just wanted to ask you something."

"We ain't buyin' nothing," the man said, starting to close the door.

"I'm not selling anything," I said quickly and with my sweetest smile. It almost made me sick to smile that way at the man who took Heidi, but I did it. "This is important," I wheedled.

"Who to, you or me?"

"Me," I said, grinning.

He relaxed a little, then, like he thought my honesty was a good joke. "Okay, I got a minute, I guess."

He pushed the door open far enough for me to squeeze in. We were in a huge room, about the size of the gym at school. It had a concrete floor, steel support beams and no ceiling, just the rusty girders of the roof two stories up. Glass-block windows along the far side and the back let in some light, although they were too thick and wavy to see through. Close to us, at my left and behind the guy, was a wall with three doors in it. Those would be the three rooms across the front of the building, closest to the street. The fourth wall of the main room, to my right, was just four huge overhead garage-type doors, all closed and bolted.

The little man turned and walked away from me, into the first of the three front rooms. I followed, guessing that I was supposed to.

It was an office, a small square room with a battered green metal desk and swivel chair, some file cabinets, a ratty old sofa along the wall. In one corner was a table with a coffeepot, hot plate, mugs, and dirty spoons and coffee grounds.

The man sat at the desk; I sat carefully on the edge of the sofa. He picked up his coffee mug and drained it, staring at me with one eye over the rim of the mug as it rose.

"Um," I began cautiously, "I was wondering if you could use some help around here for the summer. My brothers were over here yesterday looking for a dog to buy, and they told me you had a training kennel here, so I thought I'd see if I could maybe get a part-time job."

The man lowered his mug and looked at me with no great show of interest. "Nah, we don't need any help. I got a partner—he takes care of the dogs."

I nodded, as though I accepted that. "Oh well. I thought it was worth a try anyhow. You don't ask, you don't get—right?"

He warmed a little then, and the tiny mouth relaxed toward a smile.

"What do you do here?" I asked, looking around the room, "You raise dogs, or just train them, or what?"

"We buy and sell, we don't breed them. Enough other fools out there doing that. We buy cheap, train them for guard work, and sell at a profit."

At that last word his smile became genuine. I thought their profits must be good, if they were "buying" their dogs out of other people's trucks and yards when nobody was looking.

"Are they purebreds?" I asked, wanting to keep the conversation going.

"You bet. We got mostly Rotts, a few Dobes, a few Mals. They all got registration papers. Nothing but the best here."

"Could I see the dogs, if you're not too busy?"

"What you want to do that for?" He didn't sound suspicious, just lazy.

I shrugged and grinned, trying to look charming.

"I don't know. It kinda fascinates me, you know? Attack dogs. Killer dogs. It must really take guts to train those things."

"Yeah, well, my partner does the actual training and caring for the dogs. Unfortunately, I got asthma. The dog hair, you know. I'm allergic to it. So I take care of the business end of things and leave the dogs to Monte."

We sat in silence for a minute while I tried frantically, behind my bland smile, to think of something more to say so I wouldn't have to leave.

"Is it a pretty good business?" I asked finally. "I'll be out of school in four more years, so I've been thinking about what I want to do, you know, for a profession. My father wants me to go to work for him in the lawn and pool business, but I want something that's got more excitement to it. More danger, you know? Being an attack-dog trainer, that'd be neat."

He began to smile, then a thought crossed his mind and threw its shadow over his face. He looked at me through narrowed eyes. "I thought you told me those two guys that were here yesterday were your brothers."

"Yeah," I said questioningly.

"They didn't look like brothers to me. Only one of them was Mexican."

I relaxed and grinned at him. "They're my brothers. We're half Mexican, half German. It just didn't get divided very even between us. Ric looks like Mama and Hans looks like Dad."

He thought it over and apparently decided to believe me.

"Could I see the dogs?" I said again.

This time he got up and motioned to me, and I followed him into the big room. Along the left and rear walls were dog pens made of steel pipes and heavy mesh wire, seven or eight feet high. The pens weren't very big, maybe five or six feet square, with one dog to a pen. Metal feed and water buckets hung from the mesh fencing.

The first thing that hit me was the smell. The place stank of urine and wet dogs and poop. Actually the pens didn't look all that dirty. There weren't as many poop piles as I expected from the smell. The floors and walls, and the dogs themselves, were all wet or drying, as though everything had been hosed down just a little while ago. I guessed the smells were just permanent in that place. There sure wasn't much ventilation.

The office had been air-conditioned, I realized now as we left it for the hotter main room. High overhead were rows of ceiling fans that stirred the heavy air but didn't cool it.

Some of the dogs threw themselves at the fences when we walked toward them, barking and tearing at the mesh in a frenzy that scared hell out of me. Other dogs just lay on their wet floors, ignoring everything. A couple of them whirled in mad circles, wagging, or snarling, or both at the same time.

They were like zoo animals. They were nothing like my beautiful, intelligent, loving Heidi. I stared at those pens of snarling dogs and tried to picture her here. It made me sick to think about it.

Before we'd gotten to the end of the row of pens, my guide began to wheeze and hack into his handkerchief. He wasn't kidding about the asthma, or allergy or whatever. His little eyes got pink and watery and his breathing became a real fight.

Almost running, he led the way back to his air-conditioned office. Since he didn't try to get rid of me, I followed. I couldn't think of anything else to say to the guy, but I didn't want to leave. No matter what that policeman had said over the phone about not being sure about anything, I was sure. I knew these guys stole Heidi at the Bronco, I knew they'd had her here and probably sold her. And I knew there had to be records of the sales. In those file cabinets right over there along that wall was the name and address of the person who had Heidi.

All I had to do was get in with these guys enough so they'd let me hang around, then watch for my chance, and get into those files. Maybe hide out in one

of the other rooms when they left at night, or something like that.

While the little man got his breath back, I sat smiling
like an idiot, trying to get him to like me. He smiled
back, uncertainly, as though he wasn't sure why we
were doing this.

Just when the silence was getting so long that I was
afraid he'd tell me to leave so he could get back to
work, the office door opened abruptly.

Red Truck Guy stood there with a handful of mail
and a bag of groceries. He stared at me, and recog-
nition dawned.

9

"Who are you?" he demanded. "I seen you some-place before."

"Hi," I said brightly. "My name is Sox Newmann. I live around here. You probably saw me around the neighborhood, riding my bike. See, I've been looking all over town for a summer job, and yesterday my brothers came here wanting to buy a watchdog, only they wanted a shepherd and you didn't have any, but anyway they came home and—"

"Well, we ain't got no jobs for kids, so you're wasting your time hanging around here." His voice was still grouchy, but I could tell he bought my story. He came on into the office, gave the little guy the mail, and set the grocery bag down beside the coffeemaker. He poured himself a cup and loaded it with sugar.

It gave me a funny feeling, seeing the man I'd followed from a distance for so long, seeing him up close and in the open. He looked older than I'd thought. His features looked young but his skin had lots of little cracks and he was almost bald on the top of his head. His skin showed loads of acne scars, too, above the wispy beard.

He looked at me again, as though he thought I'd be gone by this time. "We don't like kids hanging around. We got important work to do and we don't like kids in the way."

The key word there was "important," and I grabbed onto it. If this jerk wanted to think he was important, then flattery might be my passport into this place.

"I can see why," I said. "Boy, if I could ever be a guard-dog trainer I sure wouldn't want other people hanging around watching me, maybe picking up my training secrets. I sure wish I had the guts to train those dogs. You must really be tough."

I was afraid that last part might have been laying it on too thick, but the guy just relaxed a little, and sipped his coffee.

"There's no big secret to it," he said. "All's you gotta do is show 'em who's boss, and you can make any dog do what you want. Knock 'em around a little bit so they respect you, and you got it made."

I had to block out the mental picture of Heidi and this man, and force my face into an eager expression.

"Listen," I said, "I know you don't like kids hanging around, but boy, if I could just watch you for a little while, if I stayed way back out of your way . . ."

He gave me a long look that warmed toward the

end. "You really go for this stuff, huh? What do you think, Valerian?"

The little bald man was absorbed in reading the mail. "I don't care," he said absently. "You're the trainer."

The man named Monte put down his mug and walked past me towards the door, motioning for me to follow.

"What's your name?" I asked him as we started across the huge echoing warehouse.

"Monte."

"Mine's Sox," I reminded him.

"What kinda name's that? Why didn't they call you 'Shoes'?" He laughed at his own wit. This guy was no mental giant, for sure. If there were any brains in this outfit, they were all in Valerian's bald little head.

As we approached the dogs, they all reacted in one way or another: either flinging themselves at the fences and snarling and biting at the wire, or cringing against the far wall.

"This one's coming along pretty good," Monte said, stopping before one of the pens. Hanging on the pen was something that looked like a short thick leash, but when Monte took it down I could see it was a pole of some kind, about two feet long, covered with leather. It had a loop on one end like a leash, and a strong snap on the other.

The dog inside was a rottweiler, as tall as Heidi but twice as broad and three times as muscular. He had a short, black coat with tan markings on head and legs, thick neck, blocky head with small evil eyes, and no tail at all that I could see.

He wore a collar that looked at first like just a heavy chain-type choke collar. But then I saw that each link of the chain had a dull spike sticking out of it, almost an inch long. The spikes pointed inward, into the dog's flesh.

Monte paused with his hand on the pen door. The dog froze and glared at him. Suddenly Monte banged the leather stick against the wire, yelling and jumping up and down while he drummed on the wire.

The dog leaped at the wire in a frenzy of barking, snarling and ripping at the wire with his teeth. The dogs in the other pens joined in.

I thought it would be suicide to open the pen gate, but Monte did just that, and instantly the Rott cringed away from him, lifting a lip in a rolling snarl but not attacking. I edged away from the open pen door.

Monte snapped the leather pole onto the spiked collar and led the dog out into the room. In the far corner was something I hadn't noticed before, a big canvas bag like a football tackle dummy. It hung by a rope from the roof girder, and it wore a man's coat.

As we got close to it, the dog began to rumble under

his breath, and to pull against his collar. I thought about those spikes digging into his throat. Either he had a terrifically high pain threshold, or he was mad enough at that dummy to want to kill it and wasn't feeling his own pain.

The dummy had a rope trailing from its bottom. Monte picked up the rope with one hand while he held back the dog with the other. Suddenly he jerked the rope. The dummy jumped toward the dog.

The dog tensed, braced, barked.

Again the dummy was jerked into a swinging dance that must have looked, to the dog, like a threatening approach. Again Monte held the dog in place.

Monte pulled the rope a third time, the dummy danced forward, and the dog lunged. This time Monte loosed his hold and yelled, "Sic 'em!"

The huge dog leaped through the air and flung himself on the dummy, his teeth sinking in just above the coat, where a man's throat would be. Snarling, jerking his head from side to side, the dog brought the dummy down to the floor and "killed" it.

The attack went on for about a minute, long enough for me to see the expression on Monte's face. It was pure excitement.

He let it go on until the dog began to lose interest, then he grabbed the dog's leather pole, dragged him back from the dummy, and handed the pole to me.

While I held the dog, Monte hoisted the dummy and hung him again by the rope. On the end of the rope was a hook that slipped through another hook on the top of the dummy; an easy breakaway so the dummy would come down as soon as the dog hit it. Like a man would.

"What'd you think of that?" Monte asked me, gloating.

"Wow," I said.

He put away the Rott and took out another dog, a malamute. She was even bigger than the rottweiler, or looked bigger because of her long, shaggy, wolf-colored coat. She had cold blue eyes set in the broad, dark mask of her head. She didn't growl at Monte, but lowered her head and walked stiff-legged beside him, the hair on the back of her neck standing straight up.

They stopped beside me. The Mal glared at me.

Monte said, "See how she raises her hackles when she's mad?" He motioned to the upright coat on the dog's neck and shoulders. "They do that when they're facing an enemy. It makes them look bigger and scarier to the enemy. Like Indians and war paint. Scare the hell out of your enemy and the fight's half over."

"She wouldn't need to bother," I said faintly. The dog looked mammoth to me, hackles or no hackles.

"Listen, tell you what," Monte said suddenly. "You

want to help? You can help. You go stand behind the dummy and shoot at her with this."

From his pocket he produced what looked like a toy gun. A water pistol, it was. I could see the water inside the clear plastic handle.

I took the pistol from him, and immediately I smelled something. I sniffed.

"Ammonia," Monte said, grinning. "Shoot for her face. A little ammonia in her eyes, and she'll be ready to tear that dummy into a million pieces. I been trying to do this with her, but it really takes two people."

I looked from the pistol to the malamute to the dummy. I did not want to do this. I did not want to be anywhere near here at this moment, period, exclamation point. This crazy man wanted me to torment a huge dog into attacking me, with only a football dummy between me and death.

But if I didn't do it, if I just handed the pistol back and said no, then Monte would lose interest in me and I'd lose my chance to get in with these guys and find Heidi. It was as simple as that. Do what Monte tells me, or forget about Heidi forever.

Swallowing, I went over to the dummy and got into position behind it.

"We'll do it three times," Monte called. "To get her riled up. I'll let her go on the third time. You get back when I let her go, but keep the dummy between you and her, so she sees it instead of you. Okay, Shoes? You're not too scared to do this?"

He was testing me. I couldn't let him know I was terrified.

"Hell no," I called back. "This is fun."

"Okay then, fire away."

I peeked around the dummy and took aim. The Mal was standing about six feet away. I didn't like her, I was scared of her, but I didn't want to hurt her. I realized suddenly that all her ferocity was a result of the way she was treated here. None of this was her fault. And here I was, about to do the same thing to her as these rotten guys had been doing.

I had to.

I took aim and pulled the trigger.

She yelped and lunged, was jerked back by her pronged collar and Monte's powerful grip on the leather pole.

I shot again. She leaped, barking furiously.

Again I shot. The instant I saw the ammonia arc toward her face I ran backwards. I tripped and fell, panicked. Rolling aside, I scrambled to my feet, but already the Mal had the dummy down and was ripping and snarling at it, just as the Rott had done.

My career as a dog trainer had begun.

10

I came back the next day, and the day after that, and pretty soon I was an accepted part of the place.

My method was a simple one: I asked questions that flattered Monte into talking nonstop, and I didn't volunteer any information about myself unless I had to. Monte and Valerian got the impression that my mother was drunk all the time and didn't know or care where I spent my days. I felt a little bad about giving that impression, especially since Mama only rarely had a glass of wine. On special occasions she'd have one, but generally she'd start giggling halfway through it and not even finish it.

But I thought it was important for Monte and Valerian to think I was on my own, and not reporting what I saw to anyone at home. I'd also given the impression that my older brothers lived in their own place, and that I didn't see much of them or Dad. I even went so far as to tell Monte a time or two that I wished I had a dad like him. When I said things like that, he'd get sort of red and pleased looking. He didn't seem to have other friends, outside of the kennel.

I began learning about him and Valerian, bit by bit. They had been brothers-in-law for a while when Valerian's sister was married to Monte. That was before she had him arrested for beating her up, and went to live in a battered wives' shelter. If there were children, Monte didn't mention them.

I thought it was odd that Valerian and Monte stayed friends through a thing like that, but when I said so to Valerian he just shrugged and said, "My sister has a voice like fingernails on a blackboard. I used to try to beat her up myself, when we were kids, but she was bigger than me."

Monte was easy enough to figure out. He was a macho jerk, and dumber than a brick. Valerian was harder to figure. His whole name, Monte told me, was Percy Joseph Valerian, but naturally he hated it and went by "P.J." or Valerian.

Monte lived in the last of the rooms across the front of the warehouse, the middle one being a large bathroom with four stalls, intended for warehouse workers. Valerian's living quarters were two small square adjoining rooms that had probably been the former warehouse boss's outer and inner offices. One held a sofa, a chair, and a small TV; the other, a bed, a dresser, and a wooden rod across one corner, where a few clothes hung.

Back when the old airport next to the warehouse was operating, the building had been used as a parcel post storage and transport area. Packages coming in by plane were stored here until they went out again by truck, or vice versa. Valerian had worked here then, as a shipping clerk.

When the airport closed and the warehouse with it, Valerian had leased the building himself. He loved the place and had been happy there. Besides, the place had almost no value with the airport gone. It was at the dead end of a residential street, and as soon as the airport closed, the zoning changed, making it impossible to do even light trucking to and from the warehouse.

The lease was even cheaper than that of Valerian's old apartment, so he'd taken it, thinking he would find some profitable use for the space, and not have to find another job.

For a while he'd rented the warehouse space to the local dog-training clubs three nights a week, for their training classes. It hadn't paid enough for Valerian to live on, but it had given him and Monte the idea to train dogs themselves for the guard-dog market and sell them at huge profits.

They'd been at it a little over a year now. Monte had worked with attack-trained dogs for a short time in Vietnam, and he had the personality for the job. Valerian took care of the advertising and selling end of it. And they were making money. Monte bragged about that.

As I became a regular, they put me to work. Monte showed me how to clean pens without going inside them, since that could be dangerous. He had a hose with a high-pressure nozzle, so the gunk could be washed out of the runs and down a floor drain with a little maneuvering of the hose. Food and water dishes were filled through the pen wire, too.

I went on helping with the "training," and hiding my hatred for it. I held dogs by the collar while Monte lashed at them with a rubber hose loaded with buck-shot. I squirted them with ammonia from behind the tackling dummy, and I yelled and prodded at them through their fence wire until they all hated me as much as they hated Monte.

I'd pedal home in the afternoons sick to my stomach at what I was seeing and doing. But with Valerian there all the time, I had no chance to get at the files, so I had to keep on these jerks' good side till I could.

One morning we sat drinking coffee in the office while Valerian read the mail. Some of the letters were inquiries about dogs for sale. Others were complaints about dogs sold in the past. From the way they talked, I guessed the complaint letters were about as common as the inquiries. I could see now why they didn't advertise their address. No one could find them here.

When he'd finished the mail Valerian said, "Monte, we're about out of blue slips. Why don't you take a run this afternoon, see if you can round up a few. We need two male Rotts, a female malamute, a couple of Dobes, if you can find them—either sex, we can use plenty of those."

I wasn't sure what they were talking about, but I thought it might be important. If I could find out something about these guys that was illegal enough to get a police warrant, then I or the police or somebody could get at the files and trace Heidi.

"Can I ride along?" I asked, and Monte said sure. He liked my company, I could tell.

We got into the red pickup and headed south out of town.

"Where are we going?" I asked finally, over the rock music.

He turned the radio down and said, "Got to get us some blue slips. We got a few contacts. You'll see."

The first place we stopped was forty miles south and east of town, in the Pedernal Hills. It was a shack on a lonely stretch of road, with a yard full of junk and a fence made of rusted hubcaps. From a long building behind it came the racket and stink of lots of dogs.

Monte left me in the truck and disappeared into the house by the back door. In five minutes he was back, an envelope in his hands and a smile on his face.

As we drove off, he handed me the envelope and I looked inside. There were two blue pieces of paper, about four by eight inches, with printing and dotted lines and signatures. I pulled them out and studied them.

They were registration application forms, from the American Kennel Club, one for a Doberman pinscher male, the other for a rottweiler male.

"I don't get it," I said.

Monte grinned down at me. "Simple. We buy blue slips off a few of these breeders and use them for our dogs when we sell them. That way we're selling AKC registerable dogs, see? We get more for them. We buy these blue slips under the table, so to speak, forty bucks apiece, and we can add two hundred bucks to the value of our dogs. Get it?"

I was beginning to. "In other words, your dogs that you have there at the kennel, you don't actually have the registration papers for those dogs, right?"

Monte winked down at me. "It's easy enough to pick up a dog when you see the chance," he said. "It's a lot harder to get the papers that go with him."

I thought of Heidi in the back of our pickup at the Bronco.

To hide my face I looked back down at the blue slips. "So what about the dogs these belong to?"

"Never existed," Monte said with relish, and slapped my knee. "These breeders, see, when they have a litter of pups, they can put down any number of puppies they want to when they register the litter, and then the American Kennel Club sends them a blue slip for each individual puppy, get it? So say the breeder's bitch has six pups. The breeder registers the litter as having nine pups, and AKC sends him nine blue slips instead of six. Then maybe one of the puppies dies, so the breeder only needs five blue slips, right? He sells the other four to me, makes a cool profit of a hundred sixty bucks, and I've got registration for some dog down the line that matches the blue slip, a mutt that looks a little like whatever breed it's supposed to be, but don't cost nothing. See how it works?"

I saw.

We went to three other kennels on a circle through Mountainair and Willard and Estancia, and back home again. We had netted five blue slips in all. Monte was pleased.

We worked our way south and west around the center of Albuquerque, staying on residential through streets but off the main highways. Monte seemed to be looking for something. He cruised along, scanning both sides of the street.

We came to a small shopping center, just a drug store and video store and a couple of other businesses. Suddenly Monte spun the truck into the parking area and pulled up behind a station wagon. In the back of the wagon was a large white dog, a German shepherd. His nose was near the top of the window, which was rolled down a few inches for ventilation.

"Sit still," Monte whispered, and in a flash he was out of the truck.

By the time I realized what he was doing he was back in the truck, peeling away before his door was even closed and laughing like a maniac.

From the back of the pickup I could hear the frantic barking and clawing of the white German shepherd.

11

I turned to peer through the dusty back window between the cab and the topper-covered rear of the truck. The dog was pacing in a circle.

"I never saw a white shepherd before," I said, trying to be cool.

"Oh yeah, they got white ones, black ones," Monte said. "We had a black one a while back. He wasn't no good, though. No guts."

He? Was Monte talking about Heidi?

"What'd you do with him?" I asked, still fighting for my cool.

"Sold him. Got an order for a shepherd, so we went ahead and shipped him—her, I guess it was. She wasn't no good, though. I never could get her to go for the dummy. No guts."

I had to turn away and look out the window, for fear of what my face might be showing.

"Hey, Shoes."

"What?"

"You're in this now, you know. You were in on this

lift, so if you were thinking about telling anybody, you just remember you're as guilty as Val and me. They lock up kids, too, you know."

"I know it."

He drove in silence, eyeing the rearview mirror. We turned south onto Forty-Seven with no sirens behind us, and Monte began to relax. I felt him watching me, so I turned to meet his gaze.

He was studying my face. "It's a kick, ain't it?" he said.

I gave him the answer he needed. "Sure is. That's the most exciting thing I ever did." I forced a grin.

"First one's always a little scary," he said in an understanding tone. "Next lift will be easier. Pretty soon you'll be doing them on your own. When you get old enough to drive, anyhow."

I swallowed and nodded.

When we got back to the kennel Monte dragged the white shepherd out of the truck and into the building.

"Hey, Val, look what we found," he called.

Valerian came to the office door and watched from there. I handed him the blue slips, which he leafed through. He smiled at them, then tossed them to the desk.

"A white one," he said, frowning at the shepherd who leaned in a crouch away from Monte. "White ones are too easy to trace. I've told you before, Monte. Just the ordinary colors. First that idiot black shepherd and now this one. Can't you stick with the sables and black-and-tans?"

I saw a look on Monte's face that I'd seen before, a smoldering resentment of Valerian's bossiness.

But I didn't care about them. All I cared about at that moment was getting away from them, getting to a phone and calling the police. There was enough here now for search warrants and arrests and convictions, enough to return the white shepherd to his owner, and all the other poor dogs leaping and yammering in their pens to theirs.

All I had to do was get out the door and onto my bike and away, without making them suspicious of me. They both were aware that, after today's action, I had enough on them to get them arrested. I may have convinced Monte that I was on their side, but he wasn't the smart one. It was Valerian I'd have to be careful of for the next little while, until I could leave without it seeming unnatural.

I stretched and yawned, preparing to say I was tired, guess I'd head home for siesta.

"You fool," Valerian snapped, cutting through my act.

They were both staring at the shepherd, who had

dropped to the floor and rolled over on his back. I knew from reading dog training books that this was a dog's way of saying, "I give in. You dominate me."

As the shepherd went belly-up, he exposed a purple mark on the inside of his thigh. I went closer and stared at it. It was a tattoo, a series of numbers written in purple ink under his skin.

"He's tattooed, you jackass," Valerian screeched, and hit Monte on the arm. "You'll have to get rid of him. Right now. Give him the shot and dump him. Can't you do anything right?"

The shot?

"No," I shouted before I could stop myself.

They turned to look at me.

"Don't shoot him. Just turn him loose."

Monte looked at me blankly, as though I were talking a foreign language. Valerian stared at me with growing suspicion.

Oh God, now I've done it.

I turned and started for the door, but Valerian darted and grabbed me. "Where're you going so fast?"

"No place. Home. I don't know."

I tried to pull away from him, but he was stronger than he looked.

"Monte!" Valerian barked.

They both had me then. Monte twisted my arm up high behind my back. I screamed with the pain.

"The police are on the way," I yelled. "I already called them."

Without stopping to realize I'd had no chance to call the police, they began to panic. Together they dragged me toward the dog pens. I fought, but I didn't have a chance.

The first pen was empty, its door swinging open. They pushed me through. There was a fast scuffle. I slipped on the wet cement and fell.

When I scrambled to my feet the pen door was shut and latched. And Valerian was inside with me.

Monte stood a few yards away, staring at us with a grin of maniacal pleasure.

"You think you're so damn smart, *Percy,* you get yourself out of that one. This whole mess is your fault. You're the one who wanted to take the kid in and teach him the business. You never could resist playing to an audience, could you? This little snot comes in off the streets and butters you up and makes you feel like a man—that's it, isn't it? You take on the kid because he listens to your bragging on yourself, and you're so stupid you never even check up on him. I always knew he was trouble, and you wouldn't even listen to me. You never did, all the time we been working together, it was always you making the decisions and me going along with them. Well, not this time. This is it, this is where I clean out the till and leave you with the mess. You wanted the kid hanging around the place—okay, you got him. I'm outta here."

He turned and ran toward the office, past the shepherd who was up and moving in uneasy circles.

Valerian stood staring at his partner, his hand clutching his throat. The wheezing was beginning.

I pushed past him and slipped my fingers through the wire mesh, straining to reach the latch. It was half an inch beyond the tips of my fingers.

Monte was back, with what looked like a big hypodermic needle filled with something white. The shepherd backed away from him.

Frantically I jumped at the fence and began to climb. It was eight feet tall, but the chain link gave me toe holds. I got to the top, got one leg over.

I teetered and almost lost my balance. The floor was incredibly far away, and concrete. If I blew it now . . .

Monte had the shepherd by the collar and was forcing the dog down to the floor.

I rolled the rest of the way over the top of the fence, and slid and fell to the floor, landing with a jarring, stinging jolt, but on my feet.

I ran and tackled Monte just as the needle was going in.

He spun on me. His hands went around my throat,

but instead of choking me, he lifted me and banged my head against the floor.

I spun away down a long, black hole.

I began feeling and hearing before I could see. There was a roar going on around me, and vibrations under me, and something hard but warm under my head.

When I opened my eyes I could see only a blur, pale in color. I hurt all over, especially my head and my throat. I concentrated on making my eyes focus, and eventually things sorted themselves out into double vision. I saw two topper roofs above me, the outlines of two back doors and of curtained windows.

I tried to sit up, but it made me so dizzy and sick to my stomach that I had to lie back down again. That was when I realized what I was lying against.

The white, still form of the shepherd.

I moved my hand up over the dog until I found the ridge of breastbone between his front legs. I felt up under the leg and thought there was a tiny pulse beating against my fingertips.

He was alive. The needle hadn't killed him. In my befuddled mind I hung onto that one fact. I didn't know where Heidi was, I didn't know if I was going to get out of this alive, myself. But somehow it was terribly important to me that this dog not be killed.

I tried again to sit up, and this time I made it. Through the front window I could see the back of Monte's head, one of his ears. Instinctively I bent low so he wouldn't see me if he looked in his mirror.

The sun was coming in from the right. We were headed south.

South. Toward the Mexican border. Monte was making a run for it.

My first reaction was relief. At the border there would be guards checking vehicles for anything illegal that might be smuggled in or out of the country. I could bang on the truck's sides and get the guards' attention.

Then I realized that between Albuquerque and the border was an awful lot of barren semi-desert where a dog and kid could be dumped and left to die in the heat. Much safer than trying to get them past the border guards.

Then Monte would be safely out of the country, and home free. If I were him, that's what I'd do.

The dog and I were going to be dumped.

I tried to focus my aching brain on the problem. What I really wanted to do was to lie down again on my doggy pillow and go back to sleep. But I knew from watching television that if you go to sleep after you get a concussion, you might die. At least I thought I'd heard that.

And if I went to sleep and let Monte dump me wherever he wanted, I might die of exposure in the sun. It was July, and it was desert.

I concentrated on the job of crawling to the back window and looking out. We were on a paved road— a narrow, patched one but still a paved road, where somebody might come along.

He wouldn't dump us here. He'd have to turn off someplace on a more deserted road, or just drive straight out over the land, to be sure of leaving us where we couldn't be found.

And that could happen any time. The landscape we were driving through was completely empty of houses. Nothing but barbed wire fence close along both sides of the road, and beyond the fences nothing but red rocky earth and clumps of greasewood and sagebrush.

Something tapped my hip. I jumped, swallowing a scream.

It was the dog's paw. He was beginning to moan and twitch. His legs paddled in a running motion.

"Don't worry," I told him softly. "I'll get us out of this."

But I didn't know how. And I was scared silly.

12

As my vision gradually cleared I concentrated on finding a way to open the back of the topper.

The topper was just a fiberglass shell the same height as the truck's cab roof. It covered the truck bed, and it had the small side windows with the nailed-down curtains stretched over them. At the back, the topper was hinged to swing up, to open over the truck's tailgate.

I glanced again through the front window at Monte's ear. Then I crawled toward the tailgate. There was a handle in the center of the topper, just above the tailgate. I turned it and pushed, and the topper door opened a few inches, letting in road-roar and dust.

I closed it again. It was too high. I'd have to open the tailgate itself, the bottom half of the barrier. If I could get the tailgate open, then I could drag and shove the dog out onto the road and jump out after him, if the truck slowed enough to make it safe.

My eyes were blurring again. I began to be aware that the heat inside the truck was intense. I wanted to push open the topper door again for air, but if I did that, and if Monte glanced back in his mirror, he'd see it.

I felt along the edges of the tailgate, trying to find a latch of some kind. Yes! They were there, one on each side. I pushed one of them down and felt the tailgate give just a fraction when I leaned against it.

I shifted to the other side, pressed down on the latch there, and leaned again. But the tailgate didn't open. It was still held in place, in the center.

The topper door latch. That was holding it. I eased the handle around again and pushed the topper door open just a fraction.

The tailgate clanged down!

I held my breath, terrified that Monte had heard the noise. But the truck went on at a steady speed. Probably he had the radio on loud, I thought with a wash of relief.

There it was, an open space a foot and a half high and probably not visible in Monte's window.

I stared at the highway flashing past, just one narrow band of highway whirling away in a blur of motion. If the dog and I rolled out now, would we survive the impact?

I didn't know. I just didn't know.

But I gripped the dog's collar and began dragging him toward the opening, just in case. I got his body lined up along the opening, and I crouched behind him, and I waited.

Road dust and exhaust fumes rolled in through the open space. I started to get dizzy again, and I couldn't see for the dust-tears in my eyes.

Suddenly I felt the truck begin to slow. I tensed.

It slowed to a near halt and swung left off the highway.

I shoved, and with a grunt the dog slipped out over the lowered tailgate and disappeared.

The truck was picking up speed now, but not too much, because of the roughness of this new road.

I stretched out lengthwise across the truck bed and rolled, not letting myself think about what I was doing.

Flashes of white and intense blue rolled past my eyes. The edge of the tailgate gouged my back as I fell over it. Earth hit my face.

I was being sucked down that long black tunnel again, but fighting it, hanging onto my pain and the light in my eyes. Monte might realize we were out of the truck. He could turn around any minute and come back for us. I had to stay awake . . .

He was there, bending over me . . . But his beard was gone and he was wearing a cap . . . like a uniform. . . .

———

The next time I woke up, the blue sky was white, and there were soft rustles and voices around me, and something very familiar in my left hand.

It was Mama's hand holding mine.

"He's awake," she said in a crying-happy voice.

Things came and went after that. I knew I was in a hospital, and that people came and did things to me from time to time. But mostly I slept.

Eventually I woke up feeling normal, except for a cast on my left leg from the knee down. Mama was always in the room when I woke up, and now I started having other visitors—the rest of the family and a policeman.

He came and sat beside the bed, and grinned down at me. "Hi, hero," he said. "Do you feel well enough to talk awhile?"

"Hero?" I said.

He pressed a button near my pillow and the bed raised up so I could see him better.

"I'm Lieutenant Derr. I'm the one you talked to on the phone, about the license number. Do you remember?"

I nodded. "What happened? Did you get them? Is the white dog . . . ?"

"We got them, thanks to you. We got a call reporting a stolen white German shepherd, and the woman said she thought she'd seen a red and white pickup. She was just coming out of the drugstore, and saw her dog was gone, and just caught a glimpse of the truck taking off.

"I remembered your report about your stolen shepherd, and I had the truck's license number, thanks to you. And also thanks to you, we had the address of the kennel. We sent a squad car out there right away. They found a Mr. Valerian locked in a dog pen and having a serious asthma attack. He said the other man had taken you and the dog, and gone off."

I was getting excited now, through all my pain. I sat up higher and said, "So you put out an APB on Monte's truck, right?"

He grinned at me again. "We alerted the highway patrol and got a helicopter out, and they picked you up just north of El Paso. The dog, too. He's at the vet's, but it looks like he'll be fine."

"Monte gave him a shot," I said, remembering.

"Baking soda."

"What?"

"He injected baking soda into the dog's lungs. It's a cheap way of killing a dog. Terribly painful. Sometimes one shot isn't enough, luckily. But it's cheaper than drugs, so that's what a lot of these unscrupulous dog dealers use."

I told him about the blue slips, and how they were bought and sold. He wrote down the names of the kennels we'd visited.

Finally, since he wasn't saying anything, I had to ask. "Did you find out where he sold my dog to? Did you look in his files?"

The officer looked down at the floor. "I'm sorry, Sox. We went through the files, but there was nothing there. They didn't keep records of their sales. Mostly the file cabinets were full of paper plates and coffee cans."

My eyes got full of tears. I couldn't help it.

Suddenly I thought of something. "Did you check in the wastebaskets or around the desk, for letters? They got lots of letters from mad customers, complaining about the dogs having whip scars or not being good watchdogs or stuff like that. Monte said Heidi didn't have any guts, so maybe her new owner wrote and complained. Would you—check that, please—please?"

He said he would, but not to count on anything. Then the nurse came and a couple of young guys rolled me onto a gurney and wheeled me away to get my ankle X-rayed.

When all the doctors and hospital people got through with me, they decided I had a medium-serious concussion, bruises and lacerations, and an ankle broken in two places. At least three days in the hospital they said, mostly to keep an eye on the concussion.

I had lots of visitors those three days, but nobody from the police, so I knew they hadn't found a letter from Heidi's owner. I had to start facing the fact that I did all that for nothing, and Heidi was never coming back.

I tried to be satisfied with what I had gained. Hans and Ric and Luther and Cruzi all made a big deal over my being a hero, and I had to admit I liked it. I knew I would never again have to prove myself, or wonder if I would be chicken in a scary situation. That was a huge relief.

Dad was mad at me for taking those chances, but I could see it was because he loved me and was having aftershocks of fear of losing me. Mama just held my hand and looked at me like I was something wonderful.

And it was great to know all the dogs got sorted out and returned to their owners, and that Monte and Valerian were in jail without bail, waiting for their trial. Lieutenant Derr told me that it was Monte's having kidnapped me that made the charges serious enough to hold him without bail. If it had just been the dog-stealing he could have got out on bail and maybe gotten away, or gotten off with a light sentence.

But kidnapping and child endangerment, that was enough to get him locked away for a very long time. I was glad.

When they finally let me out of the hospital the whole family was there to usher me through the door and into the open air. I would be on crutches till the broken ankle healed.

Hans's pickup was parked beside the curb, and behind it was a police squad car.

Mama said, "Looks like an old friend of yours is here."

I started to wave at Lieutenant Derr, but then I froze. Out of the back door of the squad car came a dog. A huge, black, wonderful, wonderful dog.

She hit me in the chest and knocked me down and scared the nurse who was walking beside me, but I didn't care. Heidi and I rolled over and over in the grass, both of us whining and crying, we were so happy.

Lieutenant Derr said as he helped me up, "You were right. We did find a complaint letter in the wastebasket. We contacted her buyer in Phoenix and explained the situation, and guaranteed him his money back, and he shipped her to us yesterday."

I looked at the grinning faces around me: Mama and Dad and Hans and Ric and Luther and Cruzi and Cruzi's husband. They were all in on the surprise.

"You guys," I said. It was all I could get out.